# HENRY'S MOON™

## Written & Illustrated
## by Geoffrey Moss

Little, Brown and Company
Boston Toronto London

First edition
**Henry's Moon**™ is a trademark of Geoffrey Moss.
Somerville House Books Ltd. is the exclusive licensee.

Library of Congress Catalog Card Number: 89-83983
ISBN: 0-316-58572-6
10 9 8 7 6 5 4 3 2 1

Produced for Little, Brown and Company
by Somerville House Books Limited
1 Eglinton Avenue East, Toronto, Ontario  M4P · 3A1

Printed in Hong Kong
Design: Design Workshop 2 Inc.

to Marion for believing in me
and to my parents

Henry was a city person. He enjoyed a lot of city things, like big stores, subways and Chinese food.

But Henry had one problem. In the city, he could hardly ever see the moon.

Things like tall buildings, thick smog, big people and crowds got in the way.

Henry wanted to see the moon every night,
so he came up with a wonderful plan.
He bought heavy cloth, some wood
and a lightbulb, and made a moon of his own.
Henry's moon was perfectly round and
it glowed. It was like magic. "Just the way
it should be," thought Henry.

Each night, Henry hung his moon inside his window and turned it on. If it rained or snowed, it didn't matter. Henry's moon still shone in his window, comforting and bright.

Time passed and Henry continued to enjoy his moon. Now and then he took it to the laundromat for washing. Sometimes he would sew a patch on it.

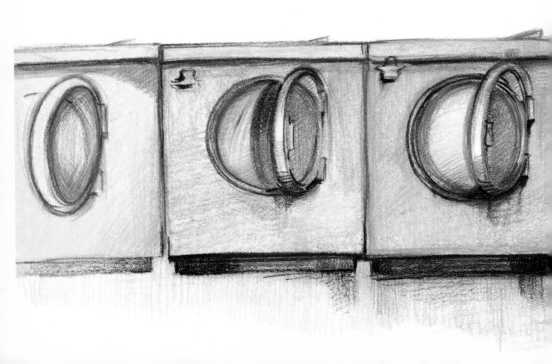

In October, Henry put an orange bulb into his moon, because he had heard that the moon was orange in October, and was called a harvest moon.

Henry had friends who lived in the country. They laughed when he told them about the moon in his bedroom. "Why not visit us and see the **real** moon?" his friends asked.

"I'll give it a try," replied Henry. "The real moon might be wonderful." So he gently stored his moon under the bed and hurried to the country.

On the first night, Henry's friends took him to the top of a hill. They pointed and said, "There, isn't that a fine moon, Henry?"

But Henry was sad. It did not look like his moon. Most of it was missing.

"Don't worry, Henry," his friends said. "Stay with us for a month, and you will see a full moon." So Henry stayed.

His friends showed him how the moon changed. One night it was just as round as his own moon. But then it got smaller and smaller...

...until it disappeared.

Henry thanked his friends for the visit. But on the train going home he thought, "What good is a moon unless it is round and glows and is there every night to make me feel good?"

As soon as he returned to his bedroom,
he took out his moon and put it in
his window. Henry turned the bulb on.
The moon was perfectly round and it glowed.

Henry stretched and yawned and as he fell asleep, he smiled. His moon would always be there. Henry's moon would always be just right for him.